D0122995

DON'T EAT THAT!

Veronika Martenova Charles

Illustrated by David Parkins

Tundra Books

Published in Canada by Tundra Books,
75 Sherbourne Street, Toronto, Ontario M5A 2P9

Published in the United States by Tundra Books of Northern New York,
P.O. Box 1030, Plattsburgh, New York 12901

Library of Congress Control Number: 2007943129

Library and Archives Canada Cataloguing in Publication

Charles, Veronika Martenova
      Don't eat that! / Veronika Martenova Charles ; illustrated by David Parkins.

(Easy-to-read spooky tales)
ISBN 978-0-88776-857-6

1. Horror tales, Canadian (English). 2. Children's stories, Canadian (English).
I. Parkins, David II. Title. III. Series: Charles, Veronika Martenova. Easy-to-read
spooky tales.

PS8555.H42242D55 2008   jC813'.54   C2007–907590–8

ONTARIO ARTS COUNCIL
CONSEIL DES ARTS DE L'ONTARIO

We acknowledge the financial support of the Government of Canada through the Book
Publishing Industry Development Program (BPIDP) and that of the Government of
Ontario through the Ontario Media Development Corporation's Ontario Book Initiative.
We further acknowledge the support of the Canada Council for the Arts and the Ontario
Arts Council for our publishing program.

Printed and bound in Canada

1 2 3 4 5 6   13 12 11 10 09 08

CONTENTS

In the Garden Part 1   4

The Fig Tree   8
(Leon's Story)

The Storm   22
(My Story)

Uncle Wolf   40
(Marcos' Story)

In the Garden Part 2   50

Afterword   55

Where the Stories Come From   56

IN THE GARDEN

PART I

"I have a job for you today,"

my mother said.

"But Leon and Marcos

are coming over," I told her.

"They can wait," she said.

"What do I have to do?" I asked.

"Cut the grass," she said.

"I'll get the lawn mower."

I waited in the garden

under a cherry tree.

The cherries were red and ripe.

I reached to pick one.

"Don't eat that!" Mom shouted,

and she gave me the lawn mower.

Soon Leon and Marcos came.

"You'll have to wait.

I won't be long," I said.

Marcos reached for a cherry.

"Don't eat that!" I yelled at him.

"Why not?" Marcos asked.

"I don't know," I answered.

"My mom said not to eat that."

"I know why," said Leon.

"It's because a small creature

might live in this cherry tree.

It could jump on you

and make you shrink.

Then you'd be small like a baby."

"What?" I said,

and stopped cutting the grass.

"Okay," said Leon.

"I'll tell you a story."

THE FIG TREE

(Leon's Story)

There was once a boy called Daku.

He lived with his tribe

in the bush.

Every time Daku went hunting

with his friends,

his grandmother would say,

"Don't eat figs!"

She said human-like creatures

lived in the fig trees.

They would catch people,

swallow them, and spit them up

over and over again.

The people got smaller each time,

until they, too,

became small creatures.

But Daku laughed at the stories.

"Such creatures don't exist,"

he would say to his friends.

"Grandma only says that

to scare me so that I'll obey."

One day, Daku and his friends

were hunting

far from their tribe's camp.

They were hot and thirsty.

Nearby, stood a big fig tree,

bent low with fruit.

"Look!" called Daku.

"Let's go and eat some!"

"No way!" said Daku's friends.

"What if some creature

does live in the treetop?

We're going back home."

Never mind, thought Daku.

All the more figs for me to eat!

Daku went to the fig tree,

picked some fruit, and ate it.

It was juicy and sweet.

WHOOSH!

Something dropped onto his back.

Daku toppled over.

A red creature with a huge head

stared at him with hungry eyes.

Its fingers and toes

were like small suction cups.

Before Daku could run,

the creature pounced on him.

Daku felt stinging pain

all over his body.

He was too weak to resist.

Opening its toothless jaw,

the creature slurped him whole,

only to spit him out seconds later.

Daku felt dizzy and strange.

Suddenly he remembered

something else Grandmother said:

The creature only eats people

if they are alive.

Daku closed his eyes

and pretended to be dead.

The creature walked around him

and poked him with a stick,

but Daku didn't move.

He lay still until night came.

Finally, the creature left

and climbed to the treetop.

Daku jumped up and ran

until he reached the camp.

"What happened?"

asked his grandmother.

"You ate some figs, didn't you?"

"How did you know?" asked Daku.

"You're smaller, that's how.

It's lucky you escaped.

Next time,

listen to what I tell you."

And from then on, Daku did.

★ ★ ★

"Wow!" said Marcos.

"Did Daku go back to kindergarten because he was so small?"

"Daku was a hunter," said Leon.

"He didn't go to school."

"I wonder if he ever got back to his normal size," I said.

"Maybe, but only if he stayed away from fig trees," said Marcos.

"I know why we should not eat these cherries," I said.

"If we eat them,

we could turn into

parrots or donkeys."

"What do you mean?" asked Leon.

"Listen to this," I said.

THE STORM

(My Story)

Avi and Ben were brothers.

Late one afternoon

they went to visit their aunt

in the next village.

Suddenly, a storm broke out.

The boys spotted a small cottage

by the road.

The door was open.

From inside, two big dogs

ran to the door, barking.

Then, two women appeared

in the doorway.

"Don't worry," they said,

and called the dogs back.

The boys thought

the women looked kind.

"Please, may we stay the night?"

Avi asked them.

"Yes," the women replied.

"Come in and have a bite to eat."

When the boys sat down at the table,

Ben noticed something strange.

One woman was stirring

boiling soup with her fingers,

while the other one

took bread from the oven

with her bare hands!

Ben was scared.

They must be witches, he thought.

The women put soup and bread

in front of the boys.

"Don't eat that!"

Ben whispered to Avi.

"I think we'd better be going,"

said Ben, pushing the food away.

"Nonsense," said one woman.

"You MUST stay.

The storm is getting worse."

She snapped her fingers,

and the dogs blocked the way.

"You can eat in the morning,"

the woman said.

Avi and Ben climbed up

to the loft, but did not sleep.

During the night they watched

through the railing to see

what the women were doing.

Around midnight,

one of the women opened the door

and sent the dogs out.

"Fetch," she said.

Moments later, four donkeys

entered the cottage.

The women took their saddles off

and the donkeys turned into men.

The monstrous dogs watched

the men carry in water

and cut wood for the fire.

Then the men were fed

soup and bread. With every bite

they looked more like donkeys.

The women put their saddles on

and the dogs herded the donkeys

into the barn.

In the morning, the women laid

soup and bread on the table.

"You MUST eat before you go,"

they ordered.

"But we are late," said Ben.

"Perhaps we could eat it

on the way," said Avi.

"All right," the women agreed.

They handed the food over.

The dogs followed the boys out.

"Thank you for the food,"

said the boys, and they ran

with the dogs racing after them.

No matter how fast the boys ran,

the dogs kept up behind them.

"The bread!" called Ben to Avi.

"Throw it!"

They threw it to the dogs.

When they turned back,

the dogs had finished the bread

and were turning into donkeys.

"Lucky we didn't eat that!"

the brothers told each other.

They kept running all the way

to their aunt's village.

But on the way back home,

they took a different path.

"I wonder what was in

that bread," said Marcos.

"I think the witches spiced it

with a potion," I said.

"They also had one for turning

people into pigs and chickens."

"I bet your mom told you

not to eat the cherries because

she is going to make you

cherry pancakes," Marcos said.

"Do you want to hear a story?

It's about a girl who was told

not to eat pancakes."

UNCLE WOLF

(Marcos' Story)

Once there was a little girl

named Bella.

One day, she asked her mother

to make her some pancakes.

But Mother was so poor,

she didn't even have a skillet.

"Go to Uncle Wolf's house

and ask him to lend us

his frying pan," said Mother.

Bella went to Uncle Wolf's house.

"What do you want?" he asked.

"Mama sent me to borrow
your skillet," said Bella.

Uncle Wolf opened the door
and gave it to her.

"Tell your mother to return it

full of pancakes," said Uncle Wolf.

When Bella reached home,

she told her mother

what Uncle Wolf had said.

Mother made two pancake stacks.

One was for Bella

and one was for Uncle Wolf.

After Bella ate her pancakes,

Mother said,

"Now, take the pan of pancakes

back to Uncle Wolf,

and don't eat any of them!"

Along the way, Bella began

to sniff the pancakes.

"They smell wonderful!

I think I will have one," she thought.

She ate one, then another.

Soon the pancakes were all gone.

So, Bella scraped some mud

from the road, patted it flat,

and made a stack of mud cakes.

She reached Uncle Wolf's house

and gave him the mud cakes.

Uncle Wolf bit into one.

"YUCK!" He spat it out.

"What is this?"

He looked at Bella and said,

"Tonight I will punish you."

Bella ran to tell her Mother

what Uncle Wolf had said.

46

Mother closed all the windows

and doors, but she forgot about

the chimney.

When night came

and Bella went to bed,

she could hear Uncle Wolf.

"I'm going to punish you.

I'm right outside!"

Then Bella heard,

CLUMP, CLUMP,

on the ceiling.

"I'm going to punish you.

I'm on the roof!"

Bella hid under the covers.

"I'm going to punish you.

I'm in the chimney!" he said.

Bella curled up in the corner.

"I'm going to punish you.

I'm in your room!"

Bella held her breath.

"Now I'm at your bed . . . !"

★   ★   ★

IN THE GARDEN

PART 2

"Leon!" shouted Marcos.

"You're not listening.

What are you doing?" he asked.

Leon was standing under the tree

squishing the fallen cherries

with his foot.

"Look! The cherries are moving!"

Leon called.

We went to take a look.

Leon was right.

The cherries were moving,

because they were full of worms.

They worms were fat and white,

and they wiggled all around.

"What's wrong?" I asked Marcos.

"I'm going to be sick," he said.

"He ate those cherries

when you were cutting grass,"

Leon told me.

My mother came into the garden.

"Aren't you finished yet?"

she asked.

"What's taking you so long?"

"Leon feels sick," I told her.

"He ate the wormy cherries."

"I should have told you about

the worms," said my mother.

"But I didn't think

you needed to hear the details.

Anyway, I made you some snacks.

Are you coming in?" she asked.

"Thanks, Mom," I said.

"But we're not very hungry now."

AFTERWORD

What do you think happens next

in Uncle Wolf's story?

How can Bella save herself?

Can she make things right?

What can she offer to do?

Have fun inventing the ending

of the story yourself.

WHERE THE STORIES COME FROM

Many folktales warn the hero

not to eat things, often fruit.

The Fig Tree is inspired by

an Australian legend

about a vampire-like being.

The Storm is from Eastern Europe,

and *Uncle Wolf* is based on

an Italian folktale. The story of

the boys eating wormy cherries

comes from my childhood. I have

remembered it to this day!